Nice Try,
Tooth Fairy

Nice Try, Tooth Fairy

By Mary W. Olson

Illustrated by Katherine Tillotson

SCHOLASTIC INC.
New York Toronto London Auckland Sydney
Mexico City New Delhi Hong Kong Buenos Aires

ISBNO-439-28817-7

Text copyright © 2000 by Mary W. Olson.
Illustrations copyright © 2000 by Katherine Tillotson. All rights reserved.
SIMON AND SCHUSTER BOOKS FOR YOUNG READERS is a trademark of Simon & Schuster.
Published by Scholastic Inc., 555 Broadway, New York, NY 10012, by arrangement with
Simon & Schuster Books for Young Readers, an imprint of Simon & Schuster Children's
Publishing Division. SCHOLASTIC and associated logos are trademarks
and/or registered trademarks of Scholastic Inc.

12 11 10 9 8 7 6 5 4 3 2 1   2 3 4 5 6 7/0

Printed in the U.S.A.   08

First Scholastic printing, January 2002

Book design by Lily Malcolm
The text for this book is set in Lemonade.
The illustrations are rendered in oil.

To my husband, Doug, and my
two boys, Eric and Michael,
for all their love and support
—M. W. O.

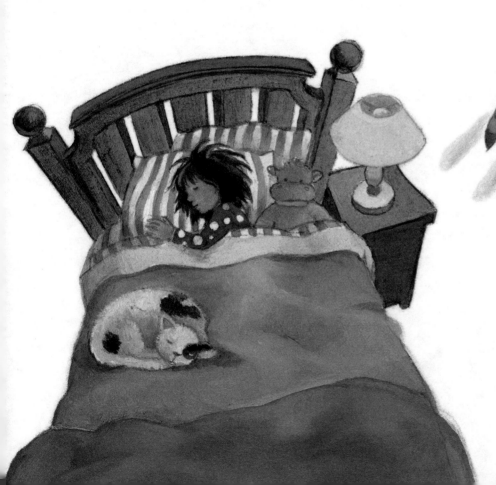

To my parents,
Henry and Elizabeth
—K. T.

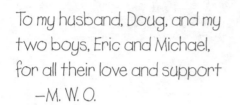

Dear Tooth Fairy,

No, my tooth isn't this small, either. I almost didn't see it under my pillow. Just as I was about to pick it up, a funny-looking creature tumbled through my window and grabbed it. I guess it was his.

Emma

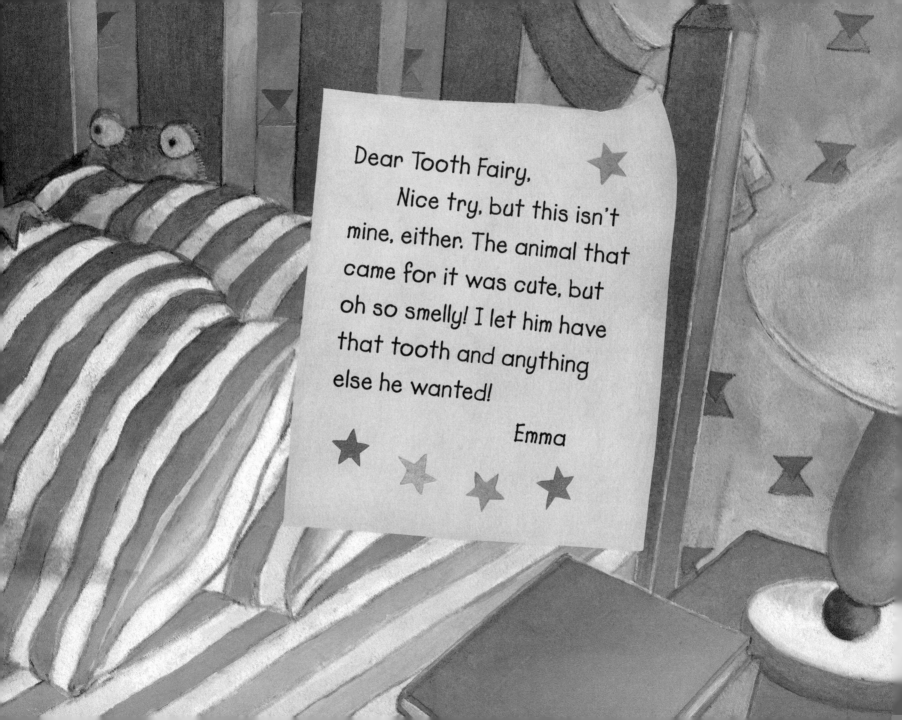

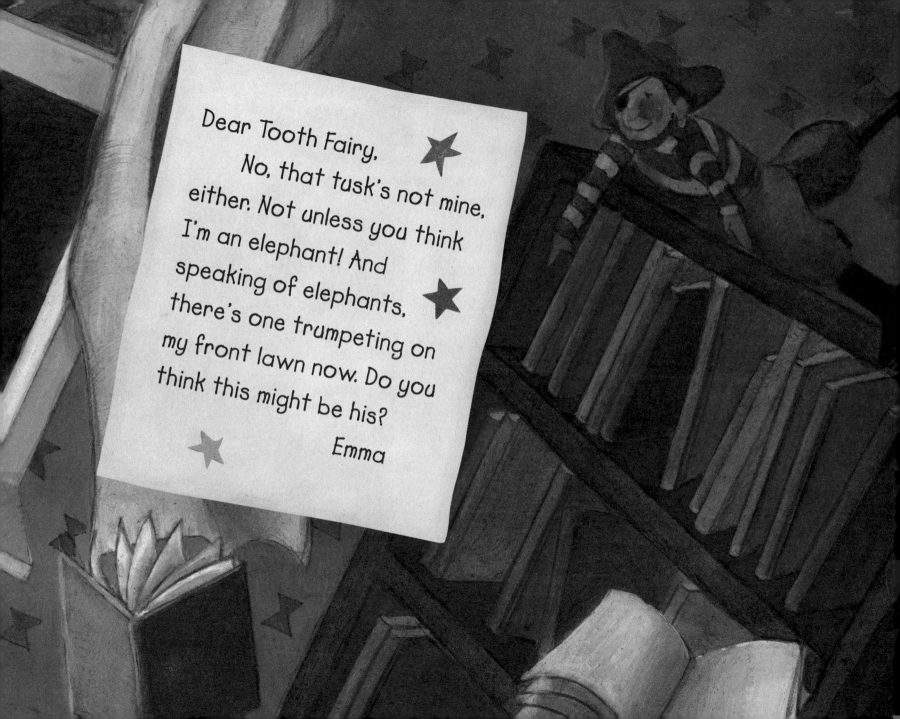

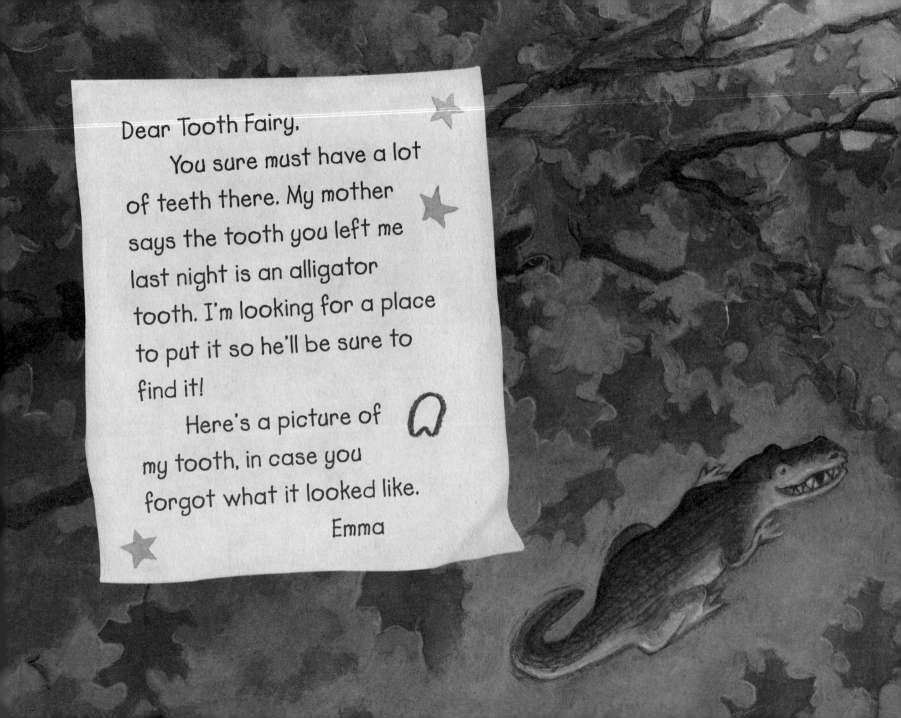

Dear Tooth Fairy,

You sure must have a lot of teeth there. My mother says the tooth you left me last night is an alligator tooth. I'm looking for a place to put it so he'll be sure to find it!

Here's a picture of my tooth, in case you forgot what it looked like.

Emma

DEAR TOOTH FAIRY.
HERE IS MY
FIRST TOOTH.
YOUR
FRIEND
HENRY